i love you more than moldy ham

CAREY F. ARMSTRONG-ELLIS

Abrams Books for Young Readers · New York

Putrid mucous, toadstool jam,
warthog waste, and moldy ham.

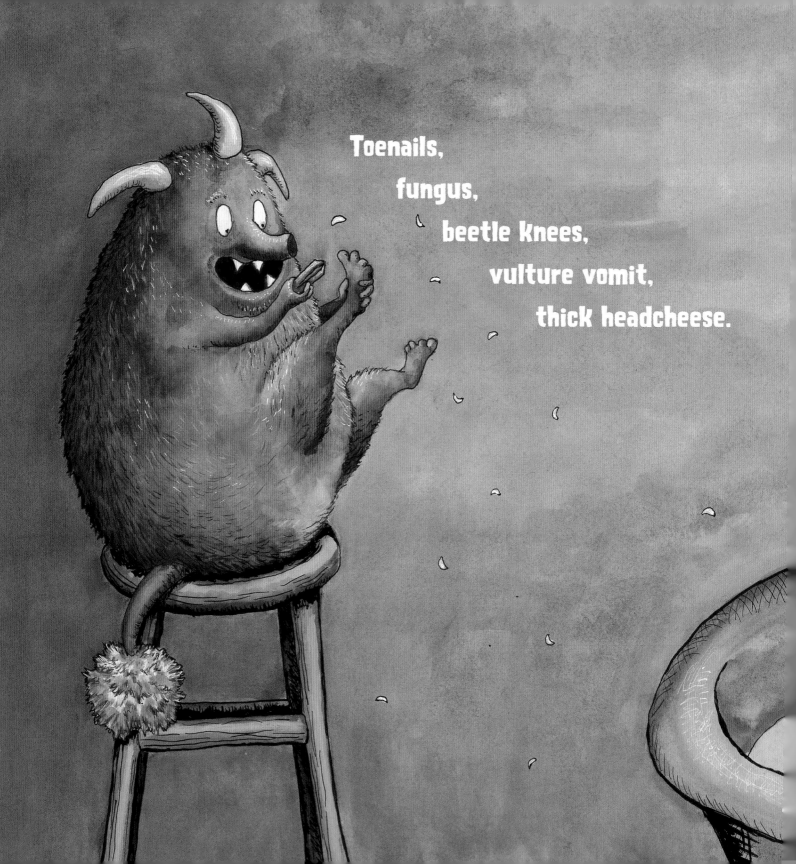

Toenails,
fungus,
beetle knees,
vulture vomit,
thick headcheese.

I love you more
than toadstool jam—
more than chunks
of moldy ham!

Climb up on a wobbly chair . . .

Woolen socks for toasty toes,
knitted mitten for my nose.
Tool belt keeps things nice and neat,
gum boots guarantee dry feet.

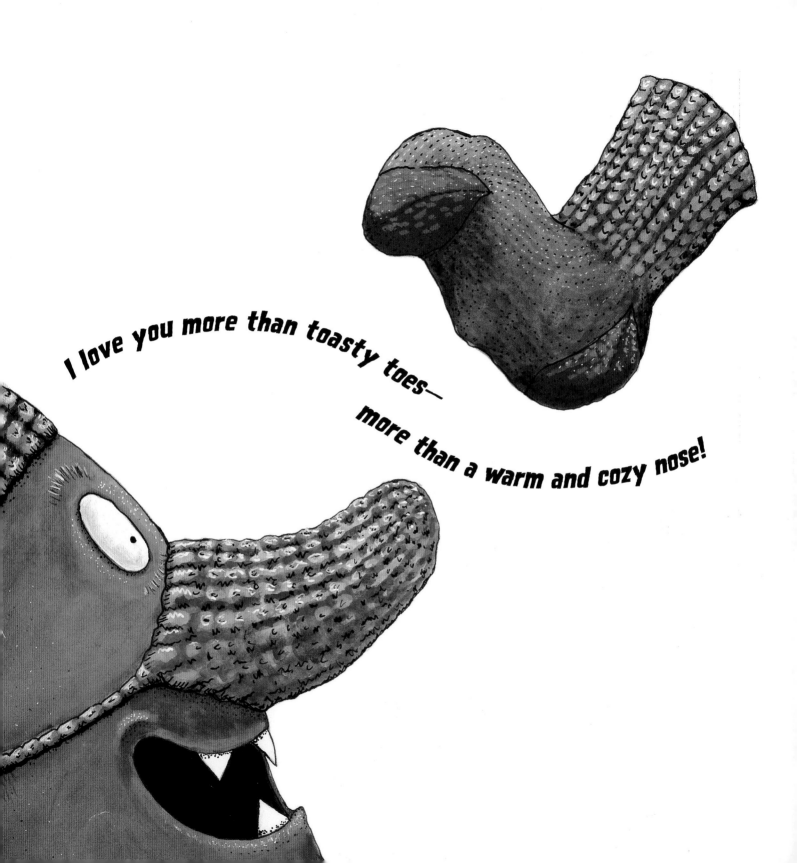

I love you more than toasty toes—
more than a warm and cozy nose!

Set out from my small abode.
Head off down the rutted road.

Hack my way through brush and briar.

Watch my step through muck and mire.

Squelchy thing squirms past my knee—
prime part of my recipe!

I love you more than mucky feet—
more than squelchy things to eat!

Sky seems strangely dark ahead . . .
Face it bravely, without dread.
Draw my trusty, well-worn sword—
battle off the hungry horde!

Home at last! I'm almost done!
Toss in plump slugs, one by one.
Prune juice goes into the mix,
chicken teeth and bloated ticks.

Dried tears from a mummy's socket,
lint balls from a dirty pocket.
Add six cups of mealworm flour.
Bake in oven for an hour.

Now it's time to decorate!

Sprinkle with
some dandruff flake.

Add some slimy nose goo drizzle;
squid squirts make a happy fizzle!

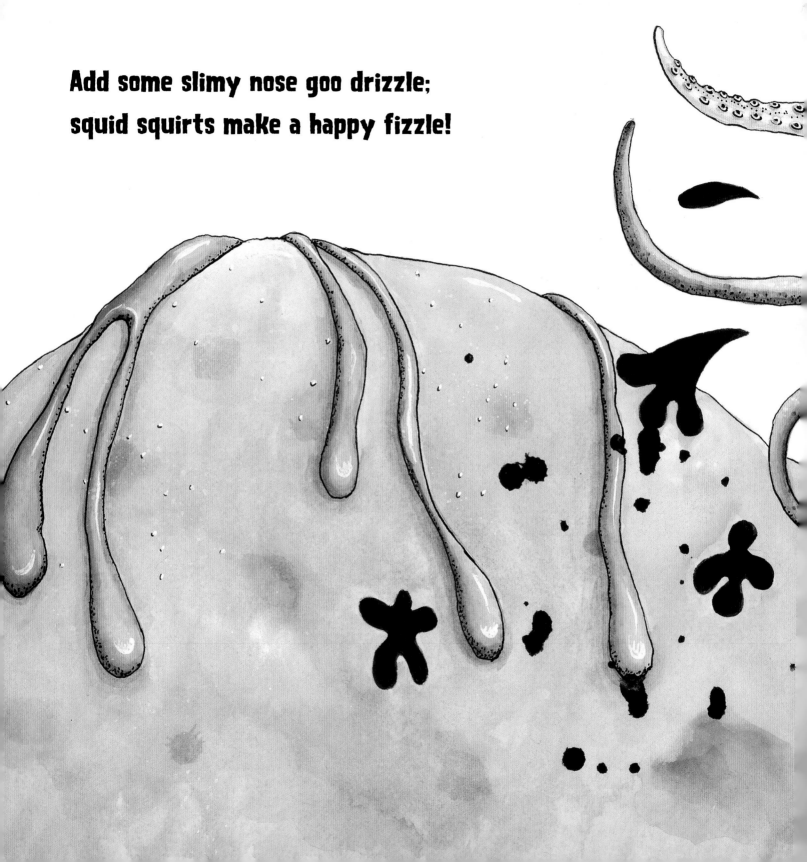

I love you more than nose goo drizzle—
more than inky squid squirt fizzle!

Behold! I've made my masterpiece,
crafted with true expertise!
Plop it on a serving tray.
It quivers as I make my way.

Reach my final destination;
enter with anticipation.
Take a peek in through the door.
Tiptoe softly 'cross the floor.

"I made you dinner, Mother dear!"
Mummy gives a happy cheer.

We squeeze each other, oozing love

(also secretions unheard of).

Happily we sit to eat.

Dinner smells like sweaty feet!

Green fog rises as we dine . . .

We dig in and life is fine.

I was delighted when my editor asked me to think about something odd, something boy-friendly, "with smelly things and squishy things and just ole yucky things" for my next book. (Of course, girls love those things as well, in my experience.) But we wanted it to have heart as well as slime. After all, monsters love their mommies too!

I would like to extend special thanks to my good friends Leonardo da Vinci, George Rodrigue, Vincent van Gogh, Mary Cassatt, Norman Rockwell, and Frederick Warren Freer. Thanks for the inspiration!

This book is dedicated to Erin and Emmy, my geeky and freaky treasures.

The pictures in this book were done with ink over gouache on 140 lb. Arches hot press paper.

Library of Congress Cataloging-in-Publication Data

Armstrong-Ellis, Carey, author, illustrator.
I love you more than moldy ham / by Carey F. Armstrong-Ellis.
pages cm
Summary: Oozing love and other secretions, a young monster prepares a putrid meal for its delighted mother.
ISBN 978-1-4197-1646-1
[1. Stories in rhyme. 2. Monsters—Fiction. 3. Cooking—Fiction.
4. Mother and child—Fiction. 5. Love—Fiction. 6. Humorous stories.] I. Title.
PZ8.3.AG33Ial 2015
[E]—dc23
2014038750

Printed and bound in China
10 9 8 7 6 5 4 3 2 1

Abrams Books for Young Readers are available at special discounts when purchased in quantity for premiums and promotions as well as fundraising or educational use. Special editions can also be created to specification. For details, contact specialsales@abramsbooks.com or the address below.

ABRAMS
THE ART OF BOOKS SINCE 1949
115 West 18th Street
New York, NY 10011
www.abramsbooks.com